CLASSIC TALES
ONCE UPON A TIME
HANSEL AND GRETEL
AF392779

ONCE UPON A TIME, THERE WERE TWO SIBLINGS, HANSEL AND GRETEL, WHO LIVED IN A VERY POOR HOUSE WITH THEIR FATHER AND STEPMOTHER.

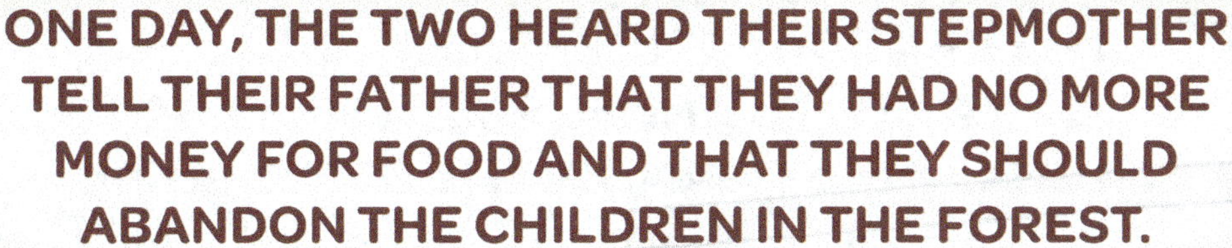

ONE DAY, THE TWO HEARD THEIR STEPMOTHER TELL THEIR FATHER THAT THEY HAD NO MORE MONEY FOR FOOD AND THAT THEY SHOULD ABANDON THE CHILDREN IN THE FOREST.

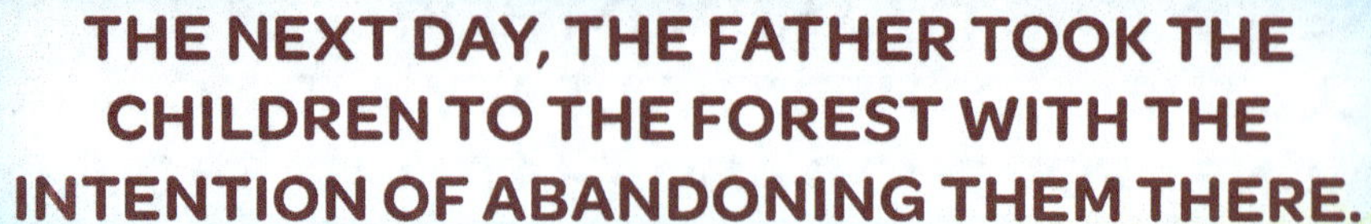

THE NEXT DAY, THE FATHER TOOK THE CHILDREN TO THE FOREST WITH THE INTENTION OF ABANDONING THEM THERE.

HE WAS VERY SAD, BUT HE THOUGHT THAT THE CHILDREN MIGHT HAVE A BETTER LIFE IF THEY WERE FOUND BY SOMEONE IN A BETTER POSITION TO RAISE THEM.

KNOWING ABOUT THEIR FATHER'S PLANS, HANSEL TOOK A PIECE OF BREAD AND STARTED SCATTERING CRUMBS ALONG THE ROAD.

THIS WAY, HE AND GRETEL COULD FIND
THEIR WAY BACK HOME.

AFTER A LONG WALK, THE THREE STOPPED UNDER A TREE TO REST. HANSEL AND GRETEL FELL ASLEEP.

WHEN THEY WOKE UP AT NIGHT, THEY REALIZED THAT THEIR FATHER HAD GONE AWAY, LEAVING THEM ALONE.

THE NEXT MORNING, THE SIBLINGS BEGAN TO SEARCH FOR THE BREADCRUMBS LEFT BY HANSEL, BUT THE BIRDS HAD EATEN EVERYTHING.

SO, THEY DECIDED TO WALK THROUGH THE FOREST IN AN ATTEMPT TO GET BACK HOME. HOWEVER, WHILE WALKING, THEY SAW A HOUSE MADE OF SWEETS.

WHEN THEY APPROACHED, A VERY KIND LADY APPEARED, OFFERING THEM FOOD. AS THEY WERE HUNGRY, THE SIBLINGS ENTERED RIGHT AWAY.

AFTER LUNCH, THE CHILDREN DECIDED TO LEAVE, BUT THE WOMAN REVEALED HERSELF TO BE A WITCH AND DID NOT ALLOW THEM TO LEAVE THE HOUSE.

THE WITCH CAPTURED HANSEL AND FORCED THE BOY TO EAT A LOT SO HE WOULD FATTEN UP, AS SHE WANTED TO BAKE HIM IN THE OVEN AND DEVOUR HIM. HOWEVER, VERY CLEVERLY, HANSEL DIDN'T EAT EVERYTHING AND ALWAYS SHOWED THE WITCH THE SAME CHICKEN BONE, DECEIVING HER. THIS WAY, HE DIDN'T GAIN WEIGHT AND MANAGED TO AVOID BEING EATEN.

ONE DAY, THE WITCH DECIDED SHE WOULD BAKE HANSEL EVEN THOUGH HE HADN'T FATTENED UP. SO, SHE ORDERED GRETEL TO LIGHT THE OVEN. AWARE OF THE WITCH'S INTENTION, THE GIRL CLAIMED SHE DIDN'T KNOW HOW TO LIGHT THE OVEN. WHEN THE WITCH OPENED THE OVEN DOOR TO TEACH HER, GRETEL PUSHED HER INSIDE AND CLOSED THE DOOR. IMMEDIATELY, SHE FREED HER BROTHER, AND BEFORE LEAVING, THEY TOOK ALL THE WITCH'S TREASURE.

AFTER A LONG WALK, HANSEL AND GRETEL
FOUND THE HOUSE WHERE THEY LIVED. WHEN
THEY ARRIVED, THEY SAW THEIR FATHER ALONE
BECAUSE THE STEPMOTHER HAD LEFT.

THE MAN HUGGED HIS CHILDREN AND EXPRESSED REGRET FOR ABANDONING THEM. THEN, WITH THE WITCH'S FORTUNE, THEY BECAME RICH AND LIVED HAPPILY EVER AFTER.

THE END